Cor

1

A Job at the Library

Mr Cutter was very angry.

'Your exam results are terrible, Tom,' he said.

'I passed my Art exam,' said Tom, 'Grade A.'

'But you've failed your History, English, Biology, Mathematics, Physics and Chemistry exams. Grade F.'

'You don't understand, Dad,' said Tom. 'I'm not interested in those subjects. I want to be an artist. I'm going to study Art and Photography at Silverton College.'

But there was bad news in a letter from Silverton College.

Silverton College, Corporation Road, Silverton, SNI INP

23 Newton Road,
Silverton,
SN5 6TF

Dear Tom
We are sorry to tell you that we cannot
offer you a place on our Art and
Photography course. We suggest that you
return to school and take your exams again.
Then you can study here next year.
Yours sincerely

David Jones

David Jones
Head of Art

And the problem was – Tom hated school. He didn't want to go back there.

'You'll have to get a job,' said Mr Cutter.

Tom was very unhappy.

'I don't want to get a job,' he said. 'I'm only seventeen. I want to draw and take photographs. One day I'll make a lot of money but —'

'Don't be stupid!' said Mr Cutter. 'When you're young you don't know what you want! Drawing is for children. You must find a job or go back to school.'

Tom wrote letters to many companies. He asked each one of them for a job. He completed forty application forms and received forty letters of rejection. There were no jobs for Tom.

Then one day he got a letter from Silverton Public Library. He had got a job as an assistant. They wanted him to start straight away.

'Excellent,' said Mr Cutter. 'This is a great opportunity. You're going to start as an assistant. But in twenty years you could be Chief Librarian.'

Tom's new job was very easy. Silverton Public Library was small and not very busy. The library was open all day, but not many people came there. They came to take books away to read at home. There were copies of newspapers in the library too. Some people came each day to read the newspapers.

Tom checked the names of the books people chose. Then he wrote down the names of the people who were borrowing the books.

Most of the time Tom sat at his desk and did nothing. He thought about the fun his friends were having at Silverton College. Most of his friends were students at the college now. They told Tom about the exciting parties they went to. Tom was very jealous. He wanted to be with his friends.

Tom sometimes drew pictures of the people who came into the library. One day a girl came into the library because it was raining. While she stood near the door Tom tried to draw her. Suddenly she turned round and saw him.

'Why are you drawing me?' she asked.

'I don't have anything to do,' he said.

The girl smiled and walked across to where Tom was sitting. She was very pretty, with dark hair ar. I brown eyes.

'I don't have anything to do either,' she said. 'I never have anything interesting to do. But sometimes I make my own clothes.'

'Did you make that coat yourself?' Tom asked. 'It looks fantastic.'

'Yes,' she said. 'I haven't got much money. I can't afford to buy the clothes I like.'

The girl's name was Rita Tatchi and she was seventeen – the same age as Tom. She did not have a job and lived with her father and her sister.

'My parents were in a car crash a few years ago,' she said. 'My mother was killed and my father was badly injured.'

'I'm sorry to hear that,' said Tom.

'Dad was once an engineer. But it's difficult for him to find work now. He's going to get some money because he was injured in the car crash. But he hasn't got the money yet.'

Rita looked around her. She saw the rows of books and

7

'Why are you drawing me?' she asked.

the table covered with newspapers and magazines. It was a very small library.

'Do you like it here?' she asked.

'It's OK,' said Tom. 'I'm paid quite well and I've got a lot to do.'

Rita moved closer to Tom and whispered. 'It's boring, isn't it?'

'All jobs are boring,' said Tom.

'No,' said Rita, 'not all jobs are boring.'

Rita looked at Tom and smiled. Tom was embarrassed. His face felt hot. He did not know what to say. Tom looked towards the window.

'I think it's stopped raining,' he said quickly. He tried to point at the window and knocked over a pile of books.

Rita laughed and began moving away. When she reached the door she turned and waved.

Tom wanted to call out to her, 'Rita, you're right. My job is boring. I hate this library. I'm an artist. I don't want a career as a librarian. I want to paint and take photographs.'

But she had gone.

2

A Great Idea

The next morning, Tom woke very early. He washed, combed his hair and put on his best clothes. When he arrived at the library he combed his hair again. Perhaps Rita would come into the library again today.

The morning passed very slowly. Very few people came into the library. In the afternoon some school children arrived. They ran around the library and made a terrible noise. One boy put chocolate on an expensive book. Tom was very angry.

At five o'clock the library closed. Tom stood at the door and looked up and down the street. He waited until six o'clock but Rita did not arrive. The next day he did the same. And the day after that.

'What's the matter with you, Tom?' his mother asked. 'Are you sick?'

'No,' said Tom. 'I'm fine.'

'Then why don't you eat your food? And you look terrible. Are you sleeping at night?'

The answer was no. Tom lay awake every night thinking of Rita. He put his drawing of her on his bedroom wall. He was in love.

Four days later, Rita returned to the library. She laughed when she saw Tom. 'You're still here,' she said. 'You're still doing this boring job.'

'I have to do this job,' said Tom.

Rita smiled. She had bright eyes and wonderful red lips. Today she was wearing a beautiful black dress.

'What do you want to do, Rita?' asked Tom.

'I want to be a fashion model,' said Rita. 'But I'm not beautiful. And I'm too short. And my nose is too big.'

'That's not true,' said Tom. 'I think you're beautiful.'

Suddenly Rita was angry.

'No, I'm not!' she said. 'I saved £300 so that I could learn to be a model. Then I went to every model agency in Silverton. None of them wanted me.'

She walked over to the table and sat down. Tom watched her pick up a magazine called *Vogue*. It was full of photos of beautiful models wearing beautiful clothes. Tom knew that Rita wanted to be one of the women in that magazine.

Tom left his desk and went over to Rita.

Rita looked up and smiled. 'I'm sorry, Tom,' she said quietly. 'I'm sorry that I shouted at you. I'm not very happy at the moment. I want to be a model very much. But nobody will help me.'

Tom understood. He wanted to go to college. He wanted to be an artist. He wanted to draw and paint all day. He wanted to go to parties at night. But he was here in this boring library.

'Rita, I think I can help you,' said Tom.

'How?'

'I can take some photos of you,' said Tom quickly. 'We can send them to all the different fashion magazines in London.'

Tom waited for Rita to say something. She looked at him very carefully. At last she said, 'I think that is a great idea, Tom.'

Tom knew that Rita wanted to be one of
the women in that magazine.

3

'Nobody Wants Me to be a Model'

The following weekend Tom and Rita went out together. Tom took his camera and they went to the park in Silverton. It was very cold. But the sun was shining brightly. They walked around the lake and the flower garden. They had lunch in the restaurant in the park. Then they sat near a big oak tree.

'I'm very happy,' said Tom.

'Me too,' said Rita. She put her hand on Tom's hand. 'I'm pleased I met you.'

They talked and talked. Then Tom took some photos of Rita wearing her new winter coat.

'I made the coat myself,' she said. 'I wanted to buy something new, but I can't afford to buy the clothes I like.'

'The coat looks wonderful,' said Tom. 'And so do you.'

'Can I take a photo of you?' asked Rita.

'Why?' asked Tom. He laughed. 'I'm not going to be a model.'

'No,' said Rita. 'But I think you're very handsome.'

Tom went red with embarrassment. 'No, I'm not,' he said.

But many girls thought Tom was handsome. He was tall and had black hair and blue eyes. And he had a very nice smile.

That night Tom developed the film he had taken of Rita. He made ten copies of the best photos of Rita. Then he sent them off to ten different fashion magazines.

On Monday he met Rita at the library. 'I've sent the

13

Many girls thought Tom was handsome. He was tall and had black hair and blue eyes.

photographs to the magazines,' he said. 'Today is 10th November. I hope they print them in the magazines before Christmas.'

Rita and Tom saw each other every day. She came into the library in the morning and read the magazines. At lunchtime, Tom gave her some of his sandwiches and his fruit juice. She told him all about the problems she had with her father.

'He wants me to marry the ugliest man in the world.'

'Why?' asked Tom.

'Because this man has money,' said Rita. 'And Dad wants me to get married to a man who has money. Dad doesn't want me to be poor all my life. But I'll only marry someone I love. And I hate Bungo.'

'Bungo! What a silly name!'

'He's a silly person. He owns a bakery and he's very, very fat. I think he eats all the cakes he makes. He has to sit on three seats when he goes on a bus.'

Tom laughed. 'Don't worry,' he said. 'Soon you'll be a famous model with a house and car of your own. You won't have to marry Bungo.'

A week later, one set of photographs was sent back. A magazine called *Fashion* did not want them.

'Don't worry,' said Tom. 'I sent sets of photos to nine other magazines.'

The next day, three more lots came back. And the day after that, five more envelopes arrived at Tom's house.

Rita was very upset. 'Nobody wants me,' she said. 'I shall never be a model.'

'No, that's not true,' said Tom. 'There's one magazine which hasn't replied yet. It's called *Dream*. Perhaps *Dream* will use our photos.'

15

A letter from *Dream* arrived the next day. It said:

DREAM

31 Holborn Street,
London,
W5

23 Newton Road
Silverton,
SN5 6TF

Dear Mr Cutter
Thank you for your photos. We think
that they are good pictures. But they are
not good enough to go in our magazine.
Why don't you learn some more about
photography. There are very good photography courses at Silverton College.
Doees Rita really want to be a model?
It is very difficult to become a model.
She will need a good agent to find work
for her. She will also need a lot of luck!

Yours sincerely

Mike Lee
Mike Lee
PS We loved the coat that Rita wore in
the photos. Does Rita know the name of
the designer?

Tom showed the letter to Rita. 'He loved your coat.
told you that your clothes were great.'

Rita started to cry.

'I don't care about the clothes. Anybody can make clothes. I want to be a model and nobody wants me.'

Tom did not know what to say. He wanted Rita to forget about becoming a model. But he was upset because she was so sad.

'Don't cry, Rita,' he said. 'We'll find you an agent.'

'But where can I find an agent?'

'I think they advertise in magazines,' said Tom.

Rita and Tom read the advertisements in all the fashion magazines in the library. They found the phone numbers of some agents. Then they phoned them. But all the agents wanted models who had worked for fashion magazines before.

Then Rita found an advertisement in the Silverton News. It said:

Models Wanted.

NO EXPERIENCE NECESSARY.

PHONE MR SPOONER TEL: 7435278.

'Look!' said Rita. 'Let's ring this number now!'

Tom was worried. He did not like the advertisement. But he did not want to upset Rita, so he said nothing.

4

The Contract

Tom and Rita met Mr Spooner in a café called Big John's.

'I'm sorry that we can't meet in my office,' said Mr Spooner. 'It's being cleaned and redecorated at the moment. But it's nice and clean in here. And the food is good.'

Tom looked around him. The café didn't look clean to him. Big John's smelt of cigarettes and cooking oil. There were dirty plates on many of the tables.

'We don't mind, do we, Tom?' said Rita.

'No, I don't think so,' said Tom slowly.

Mr Spooner was about forty. He had a bald head and a thin moustache. His suit was made of thin, shiny material and he wore a lot of gold jewellery.

'I know everyone in the fashion business,' he said. 'And I promise that you will be a top fashion model.'

Mr Spooner talked about the money Rita was going to earn. He spoke quickly and moved his hands a lot.

'In two years,' he said, 'you'll have a big house and a big car. Maybe a swimming pool.'

Tom listened in amazement. On the juke-box a song called *Smooth Operator* was playing. A smooth operator— a man who tricked people with clever words! That was Mr Spooner all right, thought Tom.

But Rita was delighted. At last, someone was telling her that she was going to be a model.

'What do I have to do?' asked Rita.

Mr Spooner looked very serious. 'It takes a long time to become a model. My fee for training you to become a model is £300. But when you start work with me you won't earn much money. Your first job will be to make coffee and sweep the floor of the office.'

Tom was very worried now, but Rita said, 'That's all right. I've got the money. I can pay you the £300.'

Mr Spooner held out some papers. 'Rita, here is a contract for you to sign. Tom, you will be a witness. You must sign the contract too. This is to say that Rita is going to work for me.'

Rita wanted to sign the contract immediately, but Tom stopped her. He picked up the contract and tried to read it. The writing was small and the words were difficult.

'I don't understand this contract,' said Tom. 'I would like to take it home and read it carefully. We'll meet you again tomorrow.'

'There are a lot of girls who want to be models,' said Mr Spooner. 'And I'm a busy man. I can't wait until tomorrow.'

'Please sign the contract, Tom,' said Rita. 'All I want to do is become a model. This is my big opportunity.'

Tom was not happy. He did not want to sign something he did not understand.

'I'm sorry,' he said to Mr Spooner, 'but I want to speak to Rita alone. Rita, please come outside with me for a moment.'

Rita followed him out of the café. She was very angry.

'Why won't you sign the contract?' she shouted.

'Because I don't trust this Mr Spooner,' said Tom. 'I don't believe what he says. I don't think that he can help you become a model.'

'You don't want me to be a model!' Rita shouted. 'You don't want me to be successful.'

*Rita wanted to sign the contract immediately,
but Tom stopped her.*

'All right!' said Tom. His face was now red with anger. 'I'll do what you want. But I think you're a fool!'

They went back into the café again. Rita signed the contract. Then Tom signed the contract.

'Write your address, please,' said Mr Spooner to Tom.

Tom did not want to give Mr Spooner his address. He did not trust Mr Spooner. So he wrote down the address of the library. Mr Spooner handed Rita another piece of paper. 'You must go to this address tomorrow morning. Bring the £300 with you. A friend of mine will tell you about your work.'

Mr Spooner pointed to the contract that Rita had signed.

'You are now working for me,' he said. 'Nobody else can take photographs of you.'

'What?' said Tom. He was beginning to hate Spooner now. 'I'm Rita's photographer!'

Mr Spooner shook his head.

'No, Tom. You aren't Rita's photographer now,' he said. He looked at his gold watch. 'I must go. I'm very busy. Goodbye.'

Rita and Tom watched Mr Spooner leave the café. Then they had another terrible argument.

'You are stupid,' said Tom. 'You only think about becoming a model. Can't you understand? Spooner is a thief!'

'So you don't want me to be a model? You want me to marry Bungo?' said Rita.

'You can marry Mickey Mouse if you want!' said Tom. 'But I don't ever want to speak to you again.'

Rita watched Tom walk away. There were tears in her eyes.

5

Looking for Rita

Tom went to work every day and sat at his desk. He was angry at first and then a little sad. Was he ever going to see Rita again? Every time the phone rang he thought it was Rita ringing. Every time a girl walked into the library he thought it was Rita.

One day, Tom's friend, Danny, came into the library. Danny had met Rita a few weeks ago.

'What's the matter, Tom?' asked Danny. 'You look terrible. And how is Rita?'

'We're not seeing each other any more,' said Tom.

'But that's crazy!' said Danny. 'You two were so happy together. What happened?'

Tom told Danny the whole story. Danny listened carefully. 'Tom, you're too proud,' he said. 'You love Rita, don't you?'

'Yes,' said Tom. 'Very much.'

'So why did you leave her? Don't you understand that this is a very difficult time for Rita? Her father wants her to marry a man she does not love. She wants a career that she cannot have.'

Tom was shocked. He had not thought about Rita's problems in this way.

'But what about Mr Spooner?' asked Tom.

Danny said, 'Mr Spooner is a bad man. He's a liar and a thief. And he knows that Rita wants someone to help her.'

'Do you think Rita hates me now?' asked Tom.

'No, I don't,' said Danny.

'What shall I do?' asked Tom.

'Phone her and say you're sorry. Tell her you love her. Give her flowers.'

'I'll think about it,' said Tom.

For the next week, Tom thought about what Danny had said. But Tom did not want to say sorry. He wanted Rita to say sorry. He was still angry.

Rita did not have a telephone. Tom did know her address, but he had never visited her home. Rita did not want her father to know about Tom. Mr Tatchi wanted Rita to marry Bungo.

At last, Tom decided to visit Rita's home. He wanted to talk to her. He still loved her very much.

Rita lived in a part of Silverton called Scrapley. It was a very poor area. People lived in big concrete buildings called tower-blocks. There was nowhere for the children to play and very few people had jobs.

Tom got off the bus and looked around him. High above, in one of the tower-blocks, some young men looked down at him.

'Why are you here? Get out!' one of the young men shouted.

A bottle smashed on the pavement in front of Tom and he felt very frightened. Everybody knew about the Scrapley 'Bad Boys'. They were very dangerous.

Tom took a piece of paper from his pocket. He looked at the paper. Rita's address was Henry Cooper House. This was the next tower-block along. Tom walked into the building. The Scrapley Boys followed him.

Tom got into the lift. Rita lived on the twenty-second floor. Tom pressed the button marked twenty-two and the lift doors closed. The Scrapley Boys banged loudly on the doors of the lift. But it was too late. The lift was moving upwards.

'I'd hate to live here,' Tom said to himself. 'I understand now why Rita wants to leave.'

Tom reached the twenty-second floor and got out of the lift. He could see all of Silverton below him. Tom could see his house and the library. Silverton College was far away in the distance. Tom could hear shouting below him. The Scrapley Boys were on the twenty-first floor. They were coming after him!

Tom hurried to flat number seven. This was where Rita and her family lived. Tom rang the doorbell and waited.

A voice called from behind the door, 'What do you want?'

'Can I speak to Rita?' asked Tom.

'Rita?' said the man behind the door. 'Rita is not here.'

'When will she return?' asked Tom.

'Never,' said the man. 'She doesn't live with us any more. She was my daughter, but now she's a stranger.'

Tom began to walk away. A girl came out of the flat and ran after him.

'Are you Tom?' asked the girl.

'Yes,' said Tom.

'My name is Shana. I'm Rita's sister.'

Shana was twelve years old. She looked like Rita. Tom knew that Rita had told Shana about him.

'Where is Rita now?' asked Tom.

Shana started to cry. 'I don't know. You upset her, Tom. And Dad wanted her to marry Bungo. So she moved out. She won't tell me where she's living.'

Suddenly the sound of shouting came from the lift.

Tom hurried to flat number seven. This was where Rita
and her family lived.

'You must leave now,' said Shana. 'The Scrapley Boys are coming. But please try and find Rita, Tom. Before it's too late!'

Shana ran back into her flat. Tom ran down the stairs. The Scrapley Boys ran after Tom.

Luckily, Tom was a fast runner.

6

A Shock for Tom

The day after he went to Rita's flat, Tom met Danny for lunch. They went to The Burger Palace across the road from the library. Danny was hungry. He ordered a cheeseburger and French fries. Then he asked for a big apple pie with ice cream. Tom only had a cup of tea.

'What can I do, Danny?' asked Tom. 'How can I find Rita? I don't know where she's living now.'

'It'll be difficult for you to find her,' said Danny. 'Do you know any of her friends?'

'No,' said Tom.

Danny finished eating his apple pie. He thought very carefully.

'There's one thing you can do,' he said, 'Think of all the places where Rita might go. Go back to the places you went to together. It's your only chance.'

Tom thanked Danny for his help and returned to work. It was December now and the weather was cold. More people came into the library because it was warm inside. Many old people liked to sit and read the newspapers. Sometimes they fell asleep.

When the library closed in the evening, Tom went to look for Rita. It was dark outside, but there were Christmas lights and decorations everywhere. In the shop windows there were signs which said: MERRY CHRISTMAS TO ALL OUR CUSTOMERS.

Tom went back to the park where he had taken the photos of Rita. But the park was closed.

It was a very cold night. Tom walked quickly to keep

warm. He passed Silverton College and saw groups of students laughing and shouting. A poster said: SILVERTON COLLEGE CHRISTMAS PARTY TONIGHT. ALL STUDENTS WELCOME.

Tom walked across the railway bridge and went into Scrapley. This was the bad area of town, but Tom did not care. He had to find Rita.

Tom came to Big John's café. Lights shone from the windows. The café looked warm inside. Tom opened the door and looked in.

The small café was full of people. The song *Smooth Operator* was playing on the juke-box again. Rita and Mr Spooner were sitting in a corner.

Rita and Mr Spooner did not see Tom. Mr Spooner was talking quickly. His arm was around Rita's shoulders.

'You have a great future,' he said. 'Today you're a poor girl from Scrapley. In a few years you'll have a big house and . . .'

Tom turned and walked out of Big John's. It was cold outside but his face was hot. There were tears in his eyes.

'Rita and Spooner!' he shouted angrily. 'Rita lied to me! She tricked me! She only wanted my help to become a model. She never liked me!'

'You have a great future,' Spooner said.

7

Tom's Christmas Present

It began to snow. The snow fell all over Silverton. It fell on the railway and on the college. It fell on Big John's and on the tower-blocks in Scrapley. It fell on the library and on The Burger Palace across the road.

Tom sat at his desk in the library. People came to him with books. They shook off the snow from their coats onto the newspapers. Children threw snow at the library windows. But Tom said nothing.

Danny came into the library. He waved at Tom but his friend did not wave back. Tom sat at the desk. He stared straight in front of him.

'Wake up, Tom,' said Danny. 'It's me, Danny.'

Tom looked up. His face was angry and unhappy. He did not smile.

'Hello, Danny,' he said at last. 'What do you want?'

Danny was upset. Tom was his best friend. They had known each other for many years. And now Tom was like a stranger.

'I haven't seen you for weeks,' said Danny. 'What have you been doing?'

'Nothing,' said Tom.

'Did you find Rita?' Danny asked.

'Yes,' said Tom. 'I found her.'

'And how is she?'

Tom's face became angry.

'I don't know,' he said. 'And I don't care. I don't ever want to see Rita again.'

Danny was shocked.

'You don't mean that, Tom,' he said.

Tom was very angry now. 'You don't know what I mean, Danny,' he said. 'You don't know anything. You're a fool. Leave me alone!'

Soon it was Christmas Eve. Everyone at the library said 'Happy Christmas' to Tom. Some people gave him Christmas cards.

Tom hated all the kindness. He did not want to see people smiling and happy. He had been happy with Rita. And now she wasn't with him any more. He loved her and he hated her at the same time. And then, suddenly, she was there. She was dressed in a new red coat and she stood at the desk in front of him. She looked more beautiful than ever.

'Hello, Tom,' she said quietly. 'Happy Christmas.'

Tom stared at her. 'What are you doing here?' he asked.

'I spoke to my sister, Shana. You went to my father's flat, didn't you?'

Tom said nothing. Rita looked so beautiful! He wanted to kiss her. But he was too angry.

'I don't live there any more,' said Rita.

'I know you don't live there any more,' Tom said angrily. 'You live with Spooner.'

'No, I don't,' said Rita. 'I live with my friend, Natalie.'

'You're a liar!' shouted Tom. 'I saw you in Big John's with Spooner.'

'Tom, I work for Spooner. I don't live with him, you idiot! I'm not his girlfriend.'

'I don't care, Rita,' said Tom. 'I want you to go away. I don't want to see you again.'

'Tom, please!' Rita started crying. A tear ran down her face. 'I need someone to talk to. I'm not happy with my job. All I do is make coffee and clean the office every day. And Spooner won't leave me alone. He says he wants to marry me.'

'Why don't you leave the job then?'

'I can't. I need the money. I have to pay the rent for the flat I share with Natalie. And I can't go back home to my father because I won't marry Bungo.'

'The library is closing now,' said Tom. 'Please leave.'

Rita held out a small package and an envelope.

'Happy Christmas,' she said.

Tom did not take the present or the card. Rita left them on the desk and walked out into the snow.

Tom picked up the package and unwrapped it. Inside was a beautiful watch. Spooner had paid for this! Another one of his tricks! Tom smashed the watch against the desk.

Then he tore the card into pieces and threw it away.

Inside the torn card there was a short message. It said: 'I love you.' The signature was Rita's.

8

An Invitation

Tom did not enjoy Christmas.

Danny was upset and did not phone him. When other friends phoned, Tom did not want to speak to them.

Tom did not go out. He did not talk to anyone. He sat in his room and painted strange pictures. He only used dark-coloured paints.

It was a grey, cold morning when Tom woke on New Year's Day.

'I must forget about Rita,' he told himself.

Tom decided to phone Danny.

'Happy New Year, Danny,' said Tom quietly.

'Happy New Year, Tom,' said Danny. 'It's great to hear from you.'

The two friends went out for a coffee together.

'I'm sorry, Danny,' said Tom. 'I was very rude to you.'

'Forget it, Tom,' said Danny.

'I do such stupid things,' said Tom. And he told Danny about the watch and the card.

'Poor Tom,' said Danny. 'Rita does love you, you know.'

'No,' said Tom sadly. 'I don't think so.'

Tom hoped that Rita did love him. But he did not want her to hurt him again. He did not know what to do.

The Christmas holiday ended and Tom went back to work. The days were short now and the nights cold and long. Tom thought a lot about his future. He decided to take his exams again. He wanted to go to Silverton College in September.

January passed. Soon it was February. On his way to the library Tom saw Valentine's Day cards in the shop windows. Tomorrow was 14th February, the day for lovers. Tom thought about sending Rita a card. But he did not know her new address.

The next morning, Tom ran downstairs to see if there was any post. There was a letter from the college. It was asking Tom to come for an interview. But there was no Valentine's Day card.

Tom caught the bus to work. Two girls were opening Valentine cards.

They were laughing. Tom sat at his desk in the library. The morning passed very slowly. Then Mr Jackson from the large Silverton Central Library came in.

'Good morning, Tom,' he said. 'I've got a card for you. It was sent to the wrong library by mistake.'

Tom saw Rita's handwriting on the red envelope. She had sent him a Valentine card after all! He tore open the envelope.

Suddenly his face went very white. 'Oh no!' he cried.

Inside the envelope was a wedding invitation. Rita and Mr Spooner were getting married on 17th April. On the back of the card was a message.

Please phone: Tel: 828 4657 (before 8 pm)

Tom was shocked and upset. This was terrible news.

'Rita is very cruel,' he thought. 'She knows that I love her. Why has she sent me this?'

Tom showed the invitation to Danny.

'I can't believe it's true,' said Danny. 'Perhaps Rita wants you to stop her getting married.'

'I can't believe that, Danny,' said Tom.

'Try and forget about Rita then,' replied Danny.

34

'There are lots of other girls in the world.'

Tom shook his head. 'But there's no one like Rita,' he said.

9

A Visitor to the Library

Tom tried to forget about Rita's wedding. He worked hard in the library during the day. He studied for many hours at night. Sometimes he tried to paint pictures.

'Rita has gone for ever,' he told himself. 'I must try to forget her.'

But Tom thought about Rita all the time. At night he dreamt about her.

On the last day of March, a middle-aged man came into the library. He wore a raincoat and a dark suit.

'Can I help you?' asked Tom.

'Yes,' said the man. 'Is there a Mr Tom Cutter here?'

'I'm Tom Cutter.'

'I'm Detective Inspector Finch from Silverton Police. Can I speak to you in private, please?'

Tom and the detective went into a little office at the back of the library.

'Why do you want to see me?' Tom asked.

The detective took some papers from his raincoat pocket.

'Have you seen these before?' he asked. He gave the papers to Tom.

Tom looked at the papers. There was his signature and the address of the library. Rita's signature was also there but not her address.

'It's my signature,' said Tom, 'and my handwriting. But I don't remember what this is.'

The detective took out a photograph.

'Do you know this man?' he said. 'He calls himself

36

many different names.'

Tom looked at the photo. It was a picture of a man with a bald head. He was wearing red glasses.

'That's Mr Spooner,' said Tom. 'But he wasn't wearing glasses when I met him.'

'Spooner, eh? He hasn't used that name before.'

'Who is he? What has he done?' asked Tom.

'His real name is Keith Dutton,' said the detective. 'He's a confidence trickster.'

'A what?'

'A man who tricks people to get money. You helped him to steal money from a bank.'

'I helped him!' said Tom. 'How?'

'You signed this paper for him. It says that if Spooner owes money to the bank, you will pay it back.'

'But I didn't say I would do that,' said Tom.

'You signed this piece of paper,' said the detective.

Tom remembered now. In the café he had signed Rita's contract. He had been a fool!

Tom told the detective what had happened.

'You have committed a crime, Tom,' said the detective. 'You signed the paper. You helped Spooner steal money from the bank.'

'But I didn't know what Spooner was going to do!' said Tom.

'If you are telling the truth, you must help us now,' said the detective. 'You must help us find Spooner and the girl.'

Tom thought for a moment. Then he had an idea.

'I don't know where they are now,' said Tom. 'But I think I can help you.'

Tom took the invitation to Rita's wedding out of a

'You signed this piece of paper,' said the detective.

drawer. Then he went over to the photocopier and made a copy of the invitation.

Tom gave the copy of the wedding invitation to the detective.

'You can arrest them at the wedding,' he said.

'Will you identify them?' asked the detective. 'Will you point to Rita and Mr Spooner for us? We must be certain that we have the right people.'

'Certainly,' said Tom. 'I will kiss Rita and shake Spooner's hand.'

'All right,' said the detective. 'Don't tell them what we are going to do. And don't try any tricks. Or we'll arrest you too.'

10

Shana

The weather was bad all through February. It was cold and it rained a lot. Every weekday, Tom sat at his desk and stared out of the window at the grey sky. He watched the rain fall onto the grey streets and buildings. He tried to forget about the detective. He tried to forget the promise he had made.

One afternoon, Shana came into the library and stood in front of Tom's desk. Her clothes were very wet from the rain. Tom felt sorry for her.

'Shana, what are you doing here?' he asked. 'Why aren't you at school?'

Shana pointed at the clock on the wall. 'It's four-thirty,' she said. 'We've finished school for the day.'

'Oh yes,' said Tom. 'I didn't know it was so late. What do you want?'

'Rita is getting married to Spooner,' said Shana.

'I know,' said Tom.

'You must stop her Tom,' said Shana. 'It's not too late. Go and talk to her.'

'No,' said Tom. 'I have a better idea.'

'What is it?' asked Shana.

'I can't tell you,' said Tom. 'It's a secret.'

Tom tried not to look at Shana. The girl looked like her sister.

'My sister loves you, Tom,' said Shana.

'Shana, you're too young to understand about love,' said Tom quickly. 'Go home and do your homework. You must work hard. Don't fail your exams like I did.'

'My sister loves you, Tom,' said Shana.

Tom watched Shana walk out of the library and into the rain. He felt very confused. But it was too late now. He had made his plans.

The night before the wedding, Tom did not sleep. He thought about the day that he and Rita had been to the park. He remembered laughing and talking with Rita. They had been so happy together.

11

The Accident

Saturday 17th April was a beautiful spring day. The sun shone and it was warm. In the gardens and the parks there were flowers everywhere. The sun shone through Tom's bedroom window.

Tom slowly went down to the kitchen. He did not eat his breakfast.

'What's the matter, Tom?' asked Mrs Cutter.

'Nothing,' said Tom.

'But you always eat a big breakfast on Saturdays,' said Mrs Cutter. 'Do you feel ill?'

Tom did not reply. He was not interested in food. He was too upset. Rita was getting married! And Tom was going to identify her to the police. He was going to betray her with a kiss.

'You must go back to bed,' said Mrs Cutter. 'And I'll get you some medicine.'

'I can't go back to bed,' said Tom. 'I've got to go to a wedding.'

Tom went back to his bedroom and sat on his bed. Did he have to go to the wedding? Perhaps he could run away? He looked at his watch. Twelve o'clock. The detective was coming at twelve. He ran to the bedroom window. No, it was too late. He couldn't get away. The detective was sitting in a car with another policeman. The car was parked in the road opposite Tom's house.

Tom put on his suit and went out of the house to meet the detective

'Do I have to identify Rita?' he asked.

'Yes,' said Detective Inspector Finch. 'Remember that you signed that paper for the bank, Tom. If you don't help me, I shall have to arrest you.'

'But I'm sure that Rita is innocent,' said Tom. 'Mr Spooner is the real criminal. He tricked Rita and —'

'I must arrest Rita and Spooner,' said the detective. 'Then the court will decide who is guilty of the crime and who is innocent.'

The invitation to Rita's wedding said: 12.45 Silverton Registry Office. The registry office was a large white building in the centre of the town. People got married in the registry office if they did not get married in a church.

'I want you to identify Rita and Spooner as they go into the registry office,' said Detective Inspector Finch. 'It's very important that Spooner doesn't escape.'

Tom was very confused. He hated Spooner and wanted to help the police arrest him. But what would happen to Rita? Tom didn't want her to get into trouble with the police. Perhaps she would go to prison?

'It will only take ten minutes to get to the registry office,' said the policeman driving the car. 'We have plenty of time.'

But, as they were driving through Silverton City Centre, there was an accident. A lorry crashed on the main road. The lorry fell across the road, blocking all the traffic in that part of the city. There were hundreds of crates of chickens on the lorry. The wooden crates broke open and chickens were running everywhere. People tried to help the lorry driver catch the chickens. Police arrived. Firefighters arrived. They all tried to catch the chickens and move the crates and the lorry.

Police arrived. Firefighters arrived. They all tried to catch the chickens and move the crates and the lorry.

'Unbelievable!' said Detective Inspector Finch. 'Why does this have to happen now?'

People laughed and cheered as the firefighters and the police tried to catch the chickens. It was very funny to watch. Detective Inspector Finch did not think it was funny. He jumped out of the car and pulled Tom with him.

'We've got to run,' said the detective, 'or we'll miss the wedding.'

Tom and the detective arrived at the registry office. Rita and Spooner were not outside the building. A large white car was parked outside the registry office. At the back of the car was a sign which said JUST MARRIED. Detective Inspector Finch spoke to the driver.

'What's happening?' he said to the chauffeur. 'Where are Rita and —'

'They're inside,' said the chauffeur. 'Getting married.'

Tom and the detective looked at each other.

'I think we're too late,' said Tom.

But the detective did not hear him. He was running into the building.

12

The Wedding

Then another car arrived outside the registry office. In it were Rita's father, Shana and Bungo.

'Dad, you're an idiot,' said Shana. 'You can't stop this wedding. Tom could stop it, but he is too proud and stupid.'

Rita's father was very upset. 'Rita must marry Bungo,' he said. 'You're the man to give her a good future, aren't you, Bungo?'

'Yes,' said Bungo, 'I need a wife to look after my house, and cook and clean for me. I want someone to work with me.'

'You need to go on a diet,' said Shana. 'You're too fat. You fill the whole back seat of this car.'

Shana got out of the car and helped her father out. Mr Tatchi was leaning on a walking-stick. He looked weak and ill, but he helped Bungo get out of the back seat.

Suddenly Shana saw Tom and the detective go into the building. 'Wait for me, Tom!' she shouted. And she ran after them.

Rita and Mr Spooner were in the registry office. They were standing in front of the registrar. The registrar was reading from a book.

'We'll wait until the wedding is over,' the detective said to Tom. 'Then we'll arrest them.'

But Tom was not listening. All he heard were the words of the registrar.

'Is there any reason why these two people cannot be married?'

Suddenly Tom jumped forward. 'Yes!' he shouted. 'This man Spooner is a criminal.'

The registrar dropped his book in astonishment. He had asked that question at hundreds of different weddings. And nobody had ever answered before. He did not know what to do. Rita turned round and stared at Tom. She started to cry. Shana, who had just come into the room, ran to her sister.

'What's happening?' said the registrar.

At that moment, the door crashed open loudly. Mr Tatchi and Bungo came into the room.

Mr Tatchi waved his walking-stick in the air. 'Stop this wedding now!' he shouted. 'Rita is coming home with me. She's going to marry my friend Bungo tomorrow.'

Mr Tatchi walked towards his daughter. Rita stepped back. 'I'm sorry, Dad,' she cried. 'But I had to leave home. I don't want to marry Bungo. I just want someone to love me!'

'Spooner doesn't love you!' shouted Tom.

The registrar put his hands to his head. 'Hundreds of weddings without a single problem,' he said. 'Why are you all doing this to me?'

Mr Tatchi took hold of Rita's left arm. She screamed. Detective Inspector Finch ran forward and pulled Rita away from her father. Tom tried to stop Spooner from escaping. Spooner hit Tom on the nose and threw him to the floor.

Then Spooner and Rita ran out of the registry office.

Bungo watched what was happening. His mouth was open and his eyes were wide in astonishment.

Spooner hit Tom on the nose and threw him to the floor.

'I don't want to marry that crazy girl!' he shouted.

Bungo ran out of the room.

Two more policemen arrived as Tom stood up.

'Have Rita and Spooner escaped?' he asked.

'Yes, they have,' said Detective Inspector Finch. 'And there's a lot of questions I want answered. I'm afraid you'll have to come with me to the police station.'

13

Success for Tom?

Tom was sitting in one of the rooms at the police station. Detective Inspector Finch was sitting opposite him. A policeman in uniform was standing near the door.

'Do you know where Rita and Spooner have gone?' asked the detective.

'I don't know,' said Tom. 'I shall never see Rita again.'

'I don't understand you. Why did you allow Spooner to take Rita from you?'

'I've been a fool,' said Tom. 'Rita needed my help and I didn't help her. My friend Danny told me I was wrong but I didn't listen. Now she's gone. And I'm going to prison.'

'Prison?'

'That's what's going to happen, isn't it? You said —'

Detective Inspector Finch smiled. 'It's OK, Tom. I'm not going to arrest you. You've been an idiot, but you're not a criminal. Spooner is the criminal.

'We believe what you told us. You weren't trying to steal money from the bank. You can go home, Tom.'

'What about Rita?'

'She must come and see us straight away. We must ask her some questions here at the police station. We can help her if she helps us. But she must get away from Spooner. Police officers are searching for her and Spooner now.

'When Spooner has been arrested you must come back,' the detective went on. 'We will want you to tell us everything in court.'

On his way out of the police station Tom passed Shana

On his way out of the police station Tom passed
Shana and Mr Tatchi.

and Mr Tatchi. She had her hand on her father's shoulder. Tears were running down Mr Tatchi's face.

'Oh, what an idiot I've been!' he said. 'I tried to make my daughter marry Bungo. And now Rita has gone and the police are looking for her.'

'Come on Dad,' said Shana. 'Let's go home.'

For the next two months Tom worked very hard. During the day, he worked in the library. At night, he studied for his exams. It was boring but Tom wanted to go to college. And studying was better than thinking about Rita.

Mr Cutter was very pleased. He was happy that Tom was studying. But Tom's mother was worried about him.

'He still looks so sad,' she said.

One day, Danny phoned Tom at work. Danny sounded very excited.

'I've got some news about Rita,' he said.

'I don't want to hear it, Danny,' said Tom quickly. 'You promised not to talk about her again.'

'But Tom—'

'Please, Danny, don't say anything.'

The summer passed slowly for Tom. He worked in the library, painted pictures and studied. In June, he took his exams. Danny tried many times to tell Tom news about Rita. But Tom did not want to listen.

At the end of August, Tom got his exam results. He had passed the exams with excellent grades. The Art and Photography teacher at the college phoned to congratulate him.

'Well done, Tom! We're delighted you've qualified for the course. We think you'll do well. You start your course next week. There's a party on Friday for all the new students.'

Later that morning, Shana came into the library. Tom saw her coming through the door. He quickly hid behind a shelf of books. He liked Shana but he did not want to hear any news of Rita. News of Rita would only make him sad.

When Shana had gone Tom returned to his desk. Shana had left him a copy of the *Silverton News*. There was a photo of Rita on the front of the newspaper. Tom saw the words SILVERTON GIRL and FASHION STAR. He threw the newspaper away. He did not want to read about Rita and Spooner.

A few minutes later, Danny came into the library. Danny had also passed his exams. He was smiling.

'So we're going to Silverton College, Tom. Fantastic, eh?'

'Yes, I suppose so,' said Tom.

'But why are you sad, Tom?' Danny asked. 'What's the matter? Aren't you pleased?'

'Yes,' said Tom quickly.

'Anyway,' said Danny, 'I've come to talk about the party.'

'The party for the new students on Friday?'

'That's right,' replied Danny. 'It's a "theme" party. Everyone will be wearing costumes. You have to dress as a famous character from a film.'

'Really?'

'Yes. And you must wear a mask to cover your face. You can only take the mask off after midnight.'

'That sounds very silly,' said Tom.

'No! I think it'll be fun,' said Danny. 'Everyone says

54

that the college parties are great. And it's a chance for us to meet the other new students.'

Tom shook his head. 'I don't enjoy parties without Rita,' he said.

'Oh, please come, Tom!' said Danny. 'Friday is your birthday. You must go out on your birthday.'

'But I haven't got a costume to wear,' said Tom. 'Which famous character from a film can I be?'

'Don't worry,' said Danny. 'I'll get you a costume. I know someone who makes clothes.'

14

'Happy Birthday, Tom!'

'Are you enjoying the party, Tom?' asked Danny.

Tom looked at his friend. Danny was dressed as Mickey Mouse. He was wearing large black ears and red trousers. Danny had a red mask on his face. Tom was wearing a black mask and a Charlie Chaplin costume – a bowler hat, a black suit, a walking-stick and big shoes.

'The party is great,' said Tom. 'There are so many great costumes. But my Charlie Chaplin costume is the best of all. It's fantastic. Where did you get it?'

Danny smiled. 'A friend gave it to me. Another new student. She's going to be one of the best young designers in the country.'

'Really?' said Tom. 'What's her name?'

But Danny did not answer Tom's question. 'I'm going to dance,' he said.

In the disco a crowd of people in strange costumes were dancing to loud music.

As Danny went to dance, a girl dressed in a beautiful ball dress came up to Tom.

'Hello,' she said, 'you must be Charlie Chaplin.'

Tom laughed. 'That's right,' he said. 'Who are you?'

'Cinderella,' said the girl. 'But I'm not like her in real life.'

Where had Tom heard that voice before?

'What do you mean?' asked Tom.

'Well, my handsome prince left me.'

'Why ?'

'He didn't know how much I loved him.'

Tom stared at Cinderella in amazement. There was something about the voice —

'I was so upset. I wanted to make him jealous. I nearly married a terrible man.'

Tom went on staring at the girl.

'Would you like to dance, Mr Chaplin?' she asked.,

'Yes . . .'

As they danced, Tom tried to think clearly. But he was more and more confused. What was happening? This girl sounded so much like ...

Suddenly the music stopped and there was an announcement: 'It's twelve o'clock. Everyone must take off their masks.'

The girl lifted the mask from her face. 'Happy birthday, Tom,' she said.

'Rita! But you went off with Spooner—'

'Wrong as usual, Tom,' said Rita. 'I never saw him again after I ran away from the registry office. The next day I went to the police. I told the detective everything I knew about Spooner. He told me Spooner was a confidence trickster. Then the detective told me how you helped the police.'

'So you became a famous model without Spooner?'

Rita laughed. 'Didn't you read the newspaper that my sister Shana left for you?'

Suddenly Tom remembered exactly what he had seen on the front of the newspaper.

SILVERTON GIRL NEW FASHION STAR. RITA TATCHI WINS 'YOUNG DESIGNER OF THE YEAR' PRIZE.

'A lot of things happened very quickly,' said Rita. 'I went back to live with my dad and my sister. Dad got the money for the car crash and we moved out of Scrapley.

The girl lifted the mask from her face.

Then I entered a fashion design competition.'

'But I thought that you wanted to be a model?'

'Not any more,' Rita said. 'I know now that I shall never be a model. I want a different career. I want to make clothes, not wear them.'

'So what are you going to do?' Tom asked.

'I'm going to study fashion design. I've still got a lot to learn. That's why I've come here to the college. One reason anyway.'

'What's the other reason?'

'I'm in love with one of the new Art and Photography students.'

Danny came over to Rita and Tom.

'You two planned this, didn't you?' said Tom. 'Rita, you designed my costume and Danny, you made me come to the party.'

Rita and Danny looked at each other and laughed.

'Well, you're eighteen today, Tom. I wanted to make it a special day,' said Danny. 'So, are you having a good birthday?'

Tom put his arm around Rita. 'I'm having a fantastic birthday, Danny,' he said.

Points for Understanding

1

1 Why can't Tom go to Silverton College?
2 Why is Mr Cutter pleased when Tom gets a job?
3 What does Tom learn about the girl who comes into the library?
4 Tom is not interested in his job at the library. What is Tom interested in?

2

1 Why does Tom dress in his best clothes to go to work?
2 Why isn't Tom sleeping at night?
3 What job does Rita want?
4 What is Tom's 'great idea'?

3

1 Why does Rita make her own clothes?
2 What does Rita's father want her to do? Why?
3 What goes wrong with Tom's 'great idea'?
4 Why do Rita and Tom look in all the fashion magazines?

4

1 Tom thinks that Mr Spooner is a 'smooth operator'. Why?
2 Tom doesn't want to sign Rita's contract. Why not?
3 What information does Tom write on the contract when he signs it?
4 Why do Tom and Rita argue after Spooner has left the café?

5

1 Danny tells Tom about Rita's problems. What does he tell Tom?
2 Why doesn't Tom want to tell Rita he is sorry?

3 'I understand now why Rita wants to leave,' says Tom. What does he mean?
4 What does Tom learn about Rita when he visits her flat in Scrapley?

6

1 Why does Tom go to Big John's café?
2 Who does he see at the café?

7

1 Why does Tom become angry with Danny?
2 How does Tom feel when he sees Rita again?
3 What does Rita tell Tom about Spooner and her job?
4 What does Tom do to his Christmas present from Rita? Why?

8

1 What does Tom do during his Christmas holiday?
2 How does Tom feel when he gets Rita's wedding invitation?
3 Why does Danny think Rita has sent the invitation?

9

1 Detective Inspector Finch comes to see Tom at the library. What does he tell Tom about Spooner?
2 'You have committed a crime, Tom,' says the detective. What does he mean?
3 How is Tom going to help Detective Inspector Finch?

10

1 Why does Shana come to talk to Tom?
2 Tom will not listen to Shana. What does he tell her?
3 Does Tom still love Rita? Give a reason for your answer.

11

1 Why is Tom upset on 17th April?
2 Tom and the detective have to run to the registry office.
   Why?
3 Where are Rita and Spooner?

12

1 Who arrives at the registry office after Tom and the
   detective?
2 The registrar dropped his book in astonishment. Why?
3 'I don't want to marry that crazy girl!' shouts Bungo. What
   has Rita done?
4 What does the detective want Tom to do now? Why?

13

1 Why does Detective Inspector Finch tell Tom that he can
   go home?
2 What does the detective say that Rita must do now?
3 Tears were running down Mr Tatchi's face. Why?
4 What does Tom do for the next two months?
5 Why does Shana bring Tom the *Silverton News*?
6 Where does Danny want Tom to go on Friday night? Why?

14

1 Tom talks to Cinderella. He does not know he is talking to
   Rita. Are there any clues to tell that he is talking to Rita?
2 What has Rita done since she ran away from the registry
   office ?
3 Rita gives Tom two reasons why she is going to study at
   Silverton College. What are her reasons?
4 How does Tom feel now?

Published by Macmillan Heinemann ELT
Between Towns Road, Oxford OX4 3PP
Macmillan Heinemann ELT is an imprint of
Macmillan Publishers Limited
Companies and representatives throughout the world
Heinemann is a registered trademark of Pearson Education, used under licence.

ISBN 978–1–4050–7272–4

Illustrated by Philip Bannister
Original cover template design by Jackie Hill
Cover photography by Alamy/N. Randall

Printed in Thailand

2014 2013 2012 2011
10   9   8   7